The History of Listening to Music

Displaying Data

Dona Herweck Rice

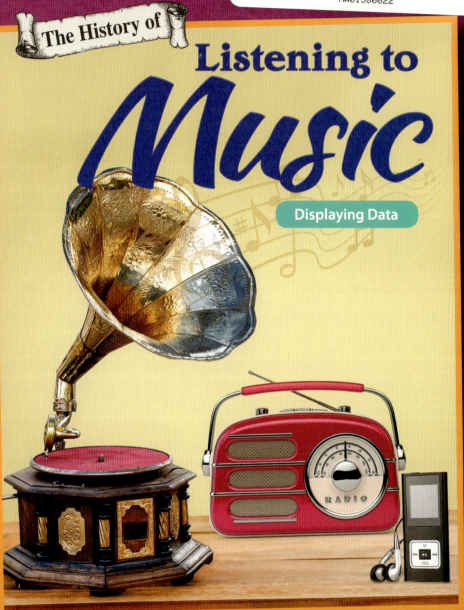

Contributing Author

Alison S. Marzocchi, Ph.D.

Consultants

Colleen Pollitt, M.A.Ed.
Math Support Teacher
Howard County Public Schools

Publishing Credits

Rachelle Cracchiolo, M.S.Ed., *Publisher*
Conni Medina, M.A.Ed., *Editor in Chief*
Dona Herweck Rice, *Series Developer*
Emily R. Smith, M.A.Ed., *Series Developer*
Diana Kenney, M.A.Ed., NBCT, *Content Director*
Stacy Monsman, M.A., *Editor*
Michelle Jovin, M.A., *Associate Editor*
Fabiola Sepulveda, *Graphic Designer*
Lee Aucoin, *Senior Graphic Designer*

Image Credits: p.6 Thomas Wyness/Shutterstock; p.7 CM Dixon Heritage Images/Newscom; p.8 Agentur/Newscom; p.9 (top) Prisma/Newscom; p.11 (left) The Trustees of the British Museum; p.11 (right) Osama Shukir Muhammed Amin FRCP/Creative Commons; p.11 (bottom), p.14 Fine Art Images Heritage Images/Newscom; p.13 (top) Lebrecht Music & Arts/Alamy; p.13 (bottom) Oronoz/Newscom; p.15 World History Archive/Newscom; p.16 Bert Hardy/Picture Post/Getty Images; p.18 (top) Library of Congress [LC-USZ62-98128]; p.18 (bottom) Library of Congress [Motion Picture, Broadcasting and Recorded Sound Division. Emile Berliner collection, 1871-1965]; p.19 (middle) B. Christopher/Alamy; p.19 (bottom) George Shuklin/Creative Commons; p.20 (middle) Joe Haupt/Creative Commons; p.20 (bottom), p.22 (top) Interfoto/Alamy; p.21 (second from top) Rybkovich/Creative Commons; p.21 (middle) Sailko/Creative Commons; p.21 (fourth from top) Atreyu/Creative Commons; p.22 (middle) Ralph Gillen/Shutterstock; p.27 (top) Warner Brothers/Getty Images; p.28 Jason Janik/Newscom; all other images from iStock and/or Shutterstock.

All companies, websites, and products mentioned in this book are registered trademarks of their respective owners or developers and are used in this book strictly for editorial purposes. No commercial claim to their use is made by the author or the publisher.

Library of Congress Cataloging-in-Publication Data

Names: Rice, Dona, author.
Title: The history of listening to music : displaying data / Dona Herweck Rice.
Description: Huntington Beach, CA : Teacher Created Materials, [2019] | Includes bibliographical references and index. |
Identifiers: LCCN 2018051881 (print) | LCCN 2018052917 (ebook) | ISBN 9781425855383 (eBook) | ISBN 9781425858940 (pbk. : alk. paper)
Subjects: LCSH: Music--History and criticism--Juvenile literature. | Mathematics--Juvenile literature.
Classification: LCC ML3928 (ebook) | LCC ML3928 .R48 2019 (print) | DDC 781.1/709--dc23
LC record available at https://lccn.loc.gov/2018051881

Teacher Created Materials
5301 Oceanus Drive
Huntington Beach, CA 92649-1030
www.tcmpub.com

ISBN 978-1-4258-5894-0
© 2019 Teacher Created Materials, Inc.
Printed in Malaysia
Thumbprints.21254

Table of Contents

World of Sound 4

History Strikes a Chord 8

Tuning In 16

Music to Our Ears 24

Problem Solving 28

Glossary 30

Index 31

Answer Key 32

World of Sound

A teen sits on a park bench with his hoodie on. The thin wires of two earbuds extend from inside his hood to his pocket, and he pats the bench beside him in a steady rhythm, matching beats that only he hears. Behind him, two preschoolers push to and fro on the swings. As they go higher and higher, they sing loudly, "Row, row, row your boat…," and then break into giggles. Down the sidewalk and alongside the park, a woman carries a black case which holds a violin. She hums a tune that has been winding through her head and is eager to get to the concert hall and play the piece with the **orchestra**. The woman is suddenly startled by a booming bass that **resonates** from a passing car with its windows down. The driver blasts modern sounds from her radio, strumming at the steering wheel like the strings of her bass guitar. The kids look up, and then they smile and sing even louder. The teen, lost in his own song, doesn't miss a beat.

LET'S EXPLORE MATH

The violinist spotted at the park is heading to an orchestra rehearsal. Imagine that there are 34 violins, 12 violas, 12 cellos, and 6 basses in the string section. The woodwind section has 5 flutes, 4 oboes, 3 clarinets, 3 bassoons, and 1 piccolo. This data is displayed in the incomplete bar graph.

1. The bar graph is missing key information. What must be added to make the display understandable?

2. Ask and answer two questions using the data in the bar graph.

Music Everywhere

Music is all around us. Nearly everywhere we go, music is being played. Whether in a restaurant, in cars, on a bus, inside a shop, or coming from smartphones, our world is filled with **melodies** and rhythms. Just try to think of a place without music. It is hard to do. And where there is no music, it is a pretty safe bet that someone would like there to be!

Archaeology shows that music has been part of human life since ancient times. Instruments of many kinds are among the common archaeological finds. But perhaps no time in history has seen such **ubiquitous** (yoo-BIH-kwih-tuhs) listening as today. Our access to music is everywhere and immediate. There are instruments, of course, just as there have always been. But computers, tablets, smartphones, and more are just a few of the ways that make listening to music today as easy as pushing buttons or plugging in.

What exactly is our history with music? Why do we listen? How do we listen? And what makes listening to music such a big deal for us all?

A band plays for a crowd of shoppers in Istanbul, Turkey.

LET'S EXPLORE MATH

Rosalie asks students in her school, "Where do you most often listen to music?" She summarizes the data in a circle graph, and students ask her questions about it. Decide whether each question can be answered only using the data in the circle graph. Answer the questions or explain why they cannot be answered.

1. How many people were surveyed?
2. Do more people listen to music at home or in the car?

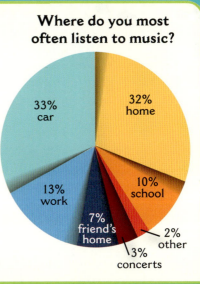

Where do you most often listen to music?

- 33% car
- 32% home
- 10% school
- 13% work
- 7% friend's home
- 3% concerts
- 2% other

People celebrate the Hindu festival of Holi with flowers, colored powder, and music.

History Strikes a Chord

There is plenty of evidence that early humans played music, and this is not surprising to find. It is clear that people enjoy music. Even babies love toy instruments—or just banging on anything handy (such as pots and pans, a table, or the floor) to make some great noise!

Some things that have been found by archaeologists and were likely used as instruments date back many thousands of years. The earliest known instruments were made of bones and other natural items. For example, hollow bones became flutes and whistles. Large shells were used as horns.

Historians believe that the first instruments were used to communicate. Hunters, for example, could whistle to one another or bang drums to gather others or to offer warnings. Even now, there are groups of people around the world who use tools like these to communicate for similar reasons.

There is no writing from these early times to suggest that people composed music. It is also unlikely they played or listened just for pleasure. But play and listen they did.

A German museum claims this is the world's oldest instrument—a flute from the Ice Age made of bone from a swan's wings.

This Roman mosaic from around 150 BC shows musicians playing a flute, cymbals, and a drum.

This Tibetan conch shell was once used as a horn.

Ancient Times

Between 2000 and 1000 BC, the emperor of China created the Imperial Office of Music. That is how important music had become! Musicians varied the **tones** of their instruments to create desired sounds. They used bells and chimes to make distinct music. They also made and used wind, string, and percussion instruments.

Ancient Greeks used math as the basis for their instruments and the sounds they created. Pythagoras found intervals in music with math. He believed the whole universe was based on numbers. The intervals found by the Greeks are the basis for the melodies used today.

Clay tablets from the 1400s BC were found in modern Syria. They include harp and voice arrangements. They also include **harmonies**. They are one of the earliest known examples of complex music that was written to be performed.

A man plays an ancient Chinese instrument.

Bowls and percussion instruments became very popular in ancient Tibet.

This reconstruction is based on a royal Mesopotamian lyre from around 2600 BC.

This clay tablet from the 1400s BC has music carved into it.

Middle Ages and Renaissance

Music in the Western world **evolved** mainly through religion. **Chanting** and **canting** were common musical styles. Music was often sacred and tied to religious experiences. Voices were more important than instruments. The songs were mainly monophonic. That means they had a single melody line. This is apparent in the chants that became popular. These Latin songs were chanted by church leaders and choirs. In some places, they are sung even today.

Music continued to evolve through the Middle Ages into the Renaissance. This is the period of time from the fall of the Roman Empire (AD 476) to about 1500. Music became polyphonic, meaning it had multiple melody lines. **Madrigals** also became popular. These were **secular** songs that were made for many voices. The lyrics to the songs were important. They were poems that were mainly about love or music itself. At this time, dance also became an important feature of music. In fact, the music was often written for the purpose of dancing.

A man plays a *rebec*—an instrument first developed during the Middle Ages.

Europeans discovered the Persian dulcimer during the Renaissance.

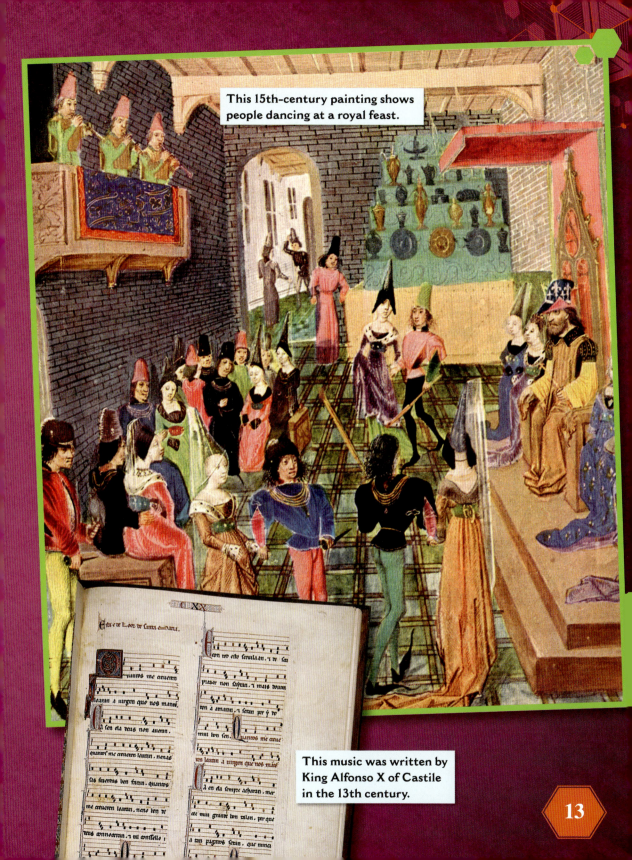

This 15th-century painting shows people dancing at a royal feast.

This music was written by King Alfonso X of Castile in the 13th century.

Baroque to Modern

Western music continued to evolve. In the baroque (buh-ROHK) period (about 1600–1750), stringed instruments were featured. Orchestras formed for the first time. Complex pieces of music were written to convey moods. Crowds gathered to hear the music played.

Music of the classical period (about 1730–1820) is lighter than Baroque music. It is also less complex, but it is not simple. It is only less complicated to the ear. People think of classical music as pleasant to listen to. A great many people still enjoy it.

This 1669 painting shows a man playing a lute while a woman sings along.

Next came the romantic period (about 1820–1910). Orchestras performed longer **symphonies**. Intense emotions could be conveyed in a single piece.

The modern era of music began about 1900. Melody grew less important than it had been. But percussion gained emphasis. Modern music is often sung and danced to a beat. A wide range of instruments is used, such as guitars, drums, and keyboards. Electronic music ushered in the widest mix of sounds ever known. There is no telling how music will evolve in the future!

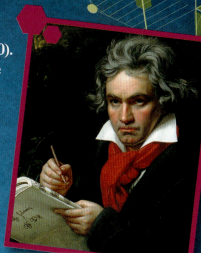

Ludwig van Beethoven was one of the most famous composers between the classical and romantic periods.

LET'S EXPLORE MATH

The Beatles were a British rock-and-roll band, considered to be one of the most innovative and influential bands of the modern era. In 1968, The Beatles shocked music listeners when they released "Hey Jude," a 7-minute single! The lengths of Beatles songs are known to vary greatly. The box plot displays data about the lengths of The Beatles' songs (in seconds) on their record, *The White Album*.

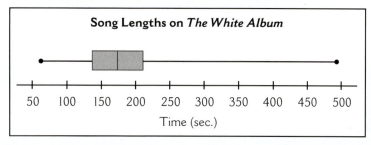

1. About how long are the shortest and longest songs?
2. Is the median song length greater or less than 4 minutes?
3. Linda claims that at least one song on *The White Album* is longer than the song "Hey Jude." Is she correct? Why or why not?

Tuning In

Just as music has changed over time, *how* people listen to it has also changed. At one time, all music was heard live. For most of history, there has been no recorded music. People only heard music as it was played or sung. They might gather around fires or sit in theaters to hear it played. Members of a family or a few people in a village may have mastered music to entertain themselves and one another. A family's evening might be spent singing or playing. A community might get together to hear someone play.

With the **Industrial Revolution** came inventions to record and play back music. The dawn of electric power pushed things even further. People did not have to know musicians or travel to concert halls to hear music. The music could easily come to them. They also had a wide range of music to listen to—whatever they liked best. Now, for most people, listening to recorded music is much more common than listening to it live.

Children in Wales listen to a record in 1950.

LET'S EXPLORE MATH

Bruce Springsteen is a rock-and-roll musician who is known for playing long concerts. He once played a concert that was over 4 hours long! He is also known for scheduling many concerts during each tour.

The data set describes the number of concerts scheduled during several of his tours:

207, 115, 140, 156, 20, 67, 107, 128, 133, 120, 40, 76, 62, 100, 84, 133, 34, 89

1. Draw a frequency table like this one. Make tallies and write frequencies for the numbers of concerts.

Number of Concerts	Tally	Frequency
0–19		
20–39		
40–59		
60–79		
80–99		
100–119		
120–139		
140–159		
160–179		
180–199		
200–219		

2. Set up a histogram like this one. Graph the data. Remember to write a title and labels. How does the frequency table help you make the histogram?

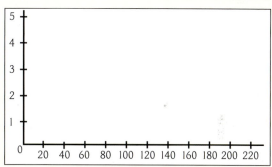

3. What claims can you make about the typical number of concerts during a Springsteen tour? Use the data to justify your answer.

Play It: The Late 1800s

The late 1800s saw a great change in how people listened to music. And the changes kept coming! Here is a look back through the evolution of devices. The journey begins with a man named Thomas Edison—one of history's most **prolific** inventors.

1877

Edison invents the phonograph. This device is used to record sound on a cylinder and play it back.

Edison wins the **patent** for the first microphone.

1881

The first headphones are used.

1887

Emile Berliner patents the gramophone. It plays music from a pre-made disk. The first disks are made of glass with grooves etched into them. A needle is used to read the grooves and play the sounds. The disks can be listened to again and again.

1896

Guglielmo Marconi invents radio **transmission**. Wireless signals begin to send sound around the world. They can be picked up and played on radio devices.

The first gramophone is sold to the public.

18

1906

Improvements are made to the phonograph. The new Victrola sells quickly despite its high price tag of $200.

1920s

In-home radio consoles come into style. Music, news, and other live programs are aired. These consoles stay in wide use until TV takes hold in the 1950s.

1925

The 78 rpm (rotations per minute) disk becomes the standard for Victrolas.

1927

Magnetic tape is invented. Sound is recorded onto the tape. Reel-to-reel players are used to play it.

1930

The first mass-produced car radio is installed.

1940s

Vinyl is used for the first time on recorded disks, or records. The $33\frac{1}{3}$ rpm LP (long-playing) record also comes into use in 1948. Vinyl LPs become the new standard.

1950s

Portable record players become popular. Record companies begin making 45 rpm records as they are more affordable for teenagers.

1954

The first transistor radios are sold. They are small radios people can carry with them. Earphones let people listen in private.

1960s

In-home stereo consoles rise in popularity. They include high-end equipment for playing records and tapes.

1963

The compact cassette is introduced. Sound is recorded onto tape inside a plastic case. A cassette player is used to play the tape.

1964

The 8-track tape is released. It is hard to listen to, as songs pause when the tracks turn over. The cassette eventually outlives the 8-track.

1970s

Large portable tape players with one or more high-powered speakers explode in popularity. They are called "boom boxes."

1979

The Sony Walkman® is released. The small, portable cassette player becomes hugely popular.

1982

The CD (compact disc) changes how music is delivered. It can hold more music than LPs or tapes. The quality of sound is more crisp and clean than the pops and scratches vinyl is known for. CDs last longer too.

1984

CD players become small and portable. The Sony Discman® becomes the follow-up to the Walkman.

1997

Music goes digital as the first MP3 players are sold. MP3 is computer **lingo**. It stands for Moving Picture Expert Groups Audio Layer 3.

2001

The Apple iPod® makes it easy to upload a huge number of music files and play them through one small device.

2005

Streaming music spikes in popularity. Pandora® launches with Spotify® following in 2007. People can listen to what they want, when they want, through their phones.

LET'S EXPLORE MATH

Jinfa asks students in the lunch line, "How many music apps do you have on your phone?" He displays the results in a dot plot.

1. How many people did Jinfa survey?

2. What are three different claims Jinfa can make about the data based on the dot plot?

3. What is a different visual display that Jinfa could use to show the same data? Why do you think this display would be a good choice?

Number of Music Apps

```
        x
        x
        x  x
        x  x
        x  x
        x  x  x
     x  x  x  x
  x  x  x  x  x        x                    x
  0  1  2  3  4  5  6  7  8  9  10
```

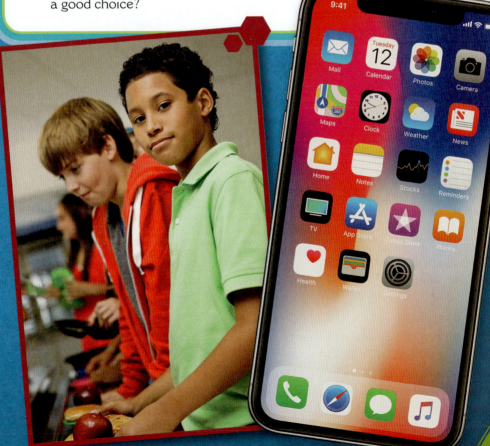

Music to Our Ears

We know that people have been listening to and making music for centuries. But why do we listen? **Statisticians** say the average American listens to about four hours of music each day. That is about one-fourth of our waking hours! Surely it is safe to say that music matters. And it is everywhere! In shopping centers, it energizes and compels us to shop more. In medical offices, it provides a calm backdrop for sensitive nerves. During tedious travel, music helps the time pass. In elevators, music makes the discomfort of riding in a small, enclosed space a bit easier on the nerves. In gyms, music motivates people to keep moving. In restaurants, loud music compels diners to eat quickly so the restaurant can seat more people per meal. In fine restaurants, soft music is often played to encourage people to linger over more food and wine—and spend more. In social settings, music fills quiet spaces and helps people feel at ease. And sometimes, music is played just to entertain.

Clearly, music serves many purposes! But perhaps one purpose stands above all others—it connects people.

LET'S EXPLORE MATH

Alfinio asks his classmates, "How many songs did you listen to today?" He uses a stem-and-leaf plot to record their responses.

Number of Songs

```
0 | 0 0 0 1 5 5
1 | 0 0 0 0 2 3 5 5 5 5 8
2 | 0 0 0 3 4 5 5 6 7 7
3 | 0 0 1 5 5
4 | 0 5
5 | 0
6 |
7 |
8 |
9 | 9
```

Key: 3 | 0 means 30 songs

1. How can you tell how many classmates Alfinio surveyed?

2. Mandy looks at the plot and says, "I see 14 zeros. That must mean that 14 people didn't listen to any music today." What is Mandy's mistake?

Community

Movie buffs know the scene well: Ilsa is in a bar, talking to Sam, the piano player. Wistfully, she says, "Play it, Sam." Recognition flashes across Sam's face. Ilsa wants him to play "As Time Goes By." But knowing the painful history that lies within the song, Sam refuses. When Ilsa asks again, he relents. As Sam plays and sings, Ilsa's former love, Rick, enters the room—and stories are told in the look that passes between him and Ilsa.

Most people can name a few songs that spark particular memories or feelings like this. Every life seems to have its own **soundtrack**! Friends and families share special songs, and music becomes a bond for them. In fact, music is often at the heart of shared experiences.

From the beginning, it seems, music has been a communal thing. People play and sing for one another or play and sing together. People share songs they love with people they love, and they dance to music with a sense of goodwill and community. Music at its best is shared, and lasting memories are made.

Whatever the history, listening to music is a truly human experience and one that bonds people together. The ways we listen may continue to change, but we will keep listening…as time goes by.

Ilsa and Rick stand while Sam plays the piano in *Casablanca*.

Problem Solving

Dave Matthews Band has some very dedicated fans! The fans maintain a website where they record information about songs played, venues, lyrics, and lengths of concerts. They use data to try to predict set lists of upcoming concerts. No doubt about it, the fans love statistics almost as much as they love music.

Imagine that you are one of the webmasters for the site. A fan emails you the question, "What is the typical length of a concert?"

The table on page 29 shows the lengths of several recent concerts. Use the data in the table to respond to the fan. Make a histogram or box plot to justify your response. Be sure to explain how the data display shows the range and typical length.

Dave Matthews performs in Dallas, Texas.

Concert	Length (minutes)
1	124
2	124
3	121
4	134
5	150
6	137
7	134
8	132
9	136
10	136
11	125
12	136
13	128
14	140
15	136
16	126
17	134
18	132
19	142

Glossary

archaeology—science dealing with the way people in the past lived

canting—a type of religious singing that is particular to the Jewish faith

chanting—a type of religious singing that is particular to the Catholic faith

evolved—changed and developed slowly over time

harmonies—combinations of different musical notes sung at the same time by different singers to create a rich sound

Industrial Revolution—period of time in the late 18th and early 19th centuries in which great advancements were made in machinery and power sources

lingo—language that is particular to a group of people

madrigals—melodious songs for many voices from 14th century Italy, usually about love or music

melodies—the notes that form the main structures of songs

orchestra—a musical group of members playing different instruments to create a unified sound

patent—a document that gives sole rights to a person or company for an invention

prolific—one who produces a lot of something

resonates—carries a loud sound for an extended time

secular—not related to religion, spirituality, or a church

soundtrack—a group of songs accompanying a movie

statisticians—people who collect and study data, or statistics

symphonies—long musical pieces performed by orchestras

tones—the pitches and vibrations of sound

transmission—the process or act of sending electronic signals, with or without wires

ubiquitous—existing everywhere

Index

ancient times, 6, 10

archaeology, 6, 8

"As Time Goes By," 26

baroque period, 14

Berliner, Emile, 18

China, 10

classical period, 14–15

community, 16, 26

devices, 18, 22

Edison, Thomas, 18

Greeks, 10

Industrial Revolution, 16

instruments, 6, 8, 10, 12, 14–15

madrigals, 12

Marconi, Guglielmo, 18

Middle Ages, 12

modern, 4, 10, 14–15

orchestra, 4–5, 14–15

recorded music, 16, 19–20

Renaissance, 12

romantic period, 15

Syria, 10

voice, 10, 12

Answer Key

Let's Explore Math

page 5
1. title; labels on axes; *y*-axis scale: 0, 10, 20, 30, 40; and instruments on *x*-axis: basses, bassoons or clarinets, cellos or violas, clarinets or bassoons, flutes, oboes, piccolos, violas or cellos, violins
2. Questions will vary. Example: *Does the orchestra have more flutes or clarinets? (flutes)*

page 7
1. cannot be answered; The total number of participants is not known.
2. car

page 15
1. shortest: about 60 seconds; longest: about 495 seconds
2. less than
3. yes; The longest song is over 8 minutes.

page 17
1. 0; 2; 1; 3; 2; 3; 4; 2; 0; 0; 1
2. Bars should match data in frequency table. Graphs should have a title and labels.
3. Claims may include that the interval of 120–140 has the most data points, and the interval of 100–120 concerts contains the median.

page 23
1. 20 people
2. Answers will vary. Example: *Most people have 2 music apps on their phones.*
3. Answers will vary. Example: *A bar graph would be a good choice because the Xs can be replaced with bars of the same height.*

page 25
1. 36; There are 36 leaves.
2. The 14 zeros are attached to stems.

Problem Solving

Example:

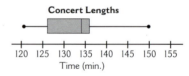

The range is 29 minutes (150 − 121 = 29). Using the medians, typical concerts will most likely be between 126 and 136 minutes.